W9-BBC-396

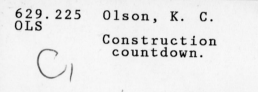

DATE			

CONSTRUCTION COUNTDOWN

CONSTRUCTION COUNT

by **K. C. Olson**

Illustrated by **David Gordon**

UCTION
DOWN

Henry Holt and Company • New York

10

Ten mighty dump trucks
rolling down the road

Nine earthmovers

9

scraping up a load

Eight bulldozers
reshaping the ground

Seven
payloaders

7

moving
dirt around

6

Six grumbling graders
leveling the land

Five heavy rollers packing down the sand

5

Four concrete mixers
turning while they travel

Three busy backhoes

scooping up
the gravel

2

Two skid loaders,
with lots of loads to haul

And one
gigantic sandbox

with room
to drive them all!

For Kirby and Aren, for starting the engine
—K. C. O.

For my dearest Susan
—D. G.

Henry Holt and Company, LLC
Publishers since 1866
115 West 18th Street
New York, New York 10011
www.henryholt.com

Henry Holt is a registered trademark of Henry Holt and Company, LLC
Text copyright © 2004 by K. C. Olson
Illustrations copyright © 2004 by David Gordon
All rights reserved.
Distributed in Canada by H. B. Fenn and Company Ltd.

Library of Congress Cataloging-in-Publication Data
Olson, K. C.
Construction countdown / by K. C. Olson; illustrated by David Gordon.
Summary: Introduces numbers and subtraction as the reader counts construction equipment from ten to one.
1. Earthmoving machinery–Pictorial works–Juvenile literature. 2. Construction equipment–Pictorial works–Juvenile literature.
3. Counting–Juvenile literature. [1. Earthmoving machinery. 2. Construction equipment. 3. Counting.]
I. Gordon, David, ill. II. Title.
TA725 .O47 2004   629.225–dc22   2003056639

ISBN 0-8050-6920-8 / First Edition–2004 / Book designed by Martha Rago and Patrick Collins
The artist used Painter 6.0 and Adobe Photoshop on a Macintosh computer to create the illustrations for this book.
Printed in the United States of America on acid-free paper. ∞

1   3   5   7   9   10   8   6   4   2